~THIS~

BOOK BELONGS

~TO~

....

....

....

~The~ PUFFIN BABY ~and~ TODDLER TREASURY

~THE~ PUFFIN BABY ~AND~ TODDLER TREASURY

PUFFIN BOOKS

VIKING/PUFFIN

Published by the Penguin Group
Penguin Books Ltd, 27 Wrights Lane, London W8 5TZ, England
Penguin Putnam Inc., 375 Hudson Street, New York, New York 10014, USA
Penguin Books Australia Ltd, Ringwood, Victoria, Australia
Penguin Books Canada Ltd, 10 Alcorn Avenue, Toronto, Ontario, Canada M4V 3B2
Penguin Books (NZ) Ltd, Cnr Rosedale and Airborne Roads, Albany, Auckland, New Zealand

Penguin Books Ltd, Registered Offices: Harmondsworth, Middlesex, England

First published 1998
5 7 9 10 8 6

First published in the United States in 2000
This edition copyright © Penguin Books Ltd, 1998
All illustrations remain the copyright © of the individual illustrators credited, 1998
The acknowledgements on page xii constitute an extension of this copyright page

Printed in Italy by L.E.G.O.

ISBN 0–670–89317–X

CONTENTS

ACKNOWLEDGMENTS

The editor and publishers gratefully acknowledge the following for permission to reproduce copyright material in this book:

'Spring Goes, Summer Comes' by Cicely Mary Barker from *Flower Fairies of the Summer* copyright © the Estate of Cicely Mary Barker, 1924, 1944, reproduced by permission of Frederick Warne & Co., illustrations by Cicely Mary Barker copyright © the Estate of Cicely Mary Barker, 1925, 1934, 1940, 1944, 1990, reproduced by permission of Frederick Warne & Co.; revised text from *The Snowman Story Book* by Raymond Briggs, first published by Hamish Hamilton Ltd 1990, revised edition published in the UK in Puffin Books 1992 and in the USA by Random House, Inc. 1990, copyright © Raymond Briggs, 1992, with additional illustrations from *The Snowman*, first published by Hamish Hamilton Ltd 1978 and in the USA by Random House, Inc. 1978, copyright © Raymond Briggs, 1978, reprinted by kind permission of the author and by arrangement with Random House, Inc.; 'Good Night' by Eleanor Farjeon from *Silver Sand and Snow*, published by Penguin Books 1992, copyright © Eleanor Farjeon, 1992, reprinted by permission of David Higham Associates; illustration by Kate Greenaway on page 126 from *Mother Goose* copyright © Frederick Warne & Co., 1985, reproduced by permission of Frederick Warne & Co.; illustrations by Elizabeth Harbour on pages 1, 37 and 176–7 from *A First Picture Book of Nursery Rhymes,* published by Viking 1995, reprinted by kind permission of the illustrator; *Spot's First Picnic* by Eric Hill copyright © Eric Hill, 1987, this presentation 1998, reproduced by permission of Ventura Publishing; *Lucy & Tom at the Seaside* by Shirley Hughes, first published by Victor Gollancz Ltd 1976, revised edition published in Puffin Books 1996, copyright © Shirley Hughes, 1976, reprinted by kind permission of the author; 'Silverly' and 'Good Night, Good Night' by Dennis Lee from *Jelly Belly*, originally published by Macmillan of Canada 1983, copyright © Dennis Lee, 1983, reprinted by kind permission of the author; 'Halfway Down' and 'Growing Up' by A. A. Milne from *When We Were Very Young*, published by Methuen Books 1924, copyright © A. A. Milne, 1924, reprinted by permission of Reed International Books and Dutton Children's Books USA, a member of Penguin Putnam, Inc., illustrations by E. H. Shepard copyright under the Berne Conventions and in the USA copyright © 1924 by E. P. Dutton, copyright renewal 1952 by A. A. Milne, colouring copyright © Dutton Children's Books USA, a member of Penguin Putnam, Inc., 1992, reprinted by permission of Curtis Brown, London; *The Tale of Tom Kitten* by Beatrix Potter copyright © Frederick Warne & Co., 1907, 1987, reproduced by permission of Frederick Warne & Co.

Grateful acknowledgment is made to *This Little Puffin*, compiled by Elizabeth Matterson, first published 1969 by Puffin Books, a publishing division of Penguin Books Ltd, revised edition published 1991. Since its first publication in 1969, *This Little Puffin* has become a classic of its kind. Parents, teachers, child-minders, playgroup leaders and many others have found it an invaluable source of rhymes, songs and games for young children.

Every effort has been made to trace copyright holders, but if there are any omissions the editor and publishers apologize for any copyright transgression and would like to hear from any copyright holders not acknowledged.

ℱOREWORD

The Puffin Baby and Toddler Treasury is both a book for babies and toddlers and a celebration of those special baby and toddler years. We also hope it will remain a precious reminder of early childhood.

While older children will enjoy poring over the wealth of stories, rhymes, and pictures it contains by themselves, the *Treasury* has been unashamedly designed as a book for adults and very young children to share. Never intended to be read from cover to cover, the emphasis in choosing the contents has been on providing a wide range of tried and tested stories and poems, all of which are short enough but satisfying enough for very young children. First words and concepts, first rhymes, first stories and first pictures – there is everything here to delight small eyes and ears and growing minds. Some popular characters and favorite illustrators also make a well-deserved appearance.

We hope *The Puffin Baby and Toddler Treasury* will bring many hours of happy reading – and many more years of happy memories.

PHILIPPA MILNES-SMITH
Publisher

Hey Diddle Diddle

Hey diddle diddle,
The cat and the fiddle,
The cow jumped over the moon;
The little dog laughed
To see such sport,
And the dish ran away with the spoon.

LITTLE MISS MUFFET

Little Miss Muffet
Sat on a tuffet,
Eating her curds and whey;
There came a big spider,
Who sat down beside her
And frightened Miss Muffet away.

Old Macdonald Had a Farm

Old Macdonald had a farm,
E-I-E-I-O!
And on that farm he had some cows,
E-I-E-I-O!
With a moo-moo here,
And a moo-moo there,
Here a moo, there a moo, everywhere a moo-moo,
Old Macdonald had a farm,
E-I-E-I-O!

Old Macdonald had a farm,
E-I-E-I-O!
And on that farm he had some sheep,
E-I-E-I-O!
With a baa-baa here,
And a baa-baa there,
Here a baa, there a baa, everywhere a baa-baa,
With a moo-moo here,
And a moo-moo there,
Here a moo, there a moo, everywhere a moo-moo,
Old Macdonald had a farm,
E-I-E-I-O!

Old Macdonald had a farm,
E-I-E-I-O!
And on that farm he had some ducks,
E-I-E-I-O!

With a quack-quack here,
And a quack-quack there,
Here a quack, there a quack, everywhere a quack-quack,
With a baa-baa here,
And a baa-baa there,
Here a baa, there a baa, everywhere a baa-baa,
With a moo-moo here,
And a moo-moo there,
Here a moo, there a moo, everywhere a moo-moo,
Old Macdonald had a farm,
E-I-E-I-O!

Old Macdonald had a farm,
E-I-E-I-O!
And on that farm he had some hens,
E-I-E-I-O!

With a cluck-cluck here,
And a cluck-cluck there,
Here a cluck, there a cluck, everywhere a cluck-cluck,
With a quack-quack here,
And a quack-quack there,

Here a quack, there a quack, everywhere a quack-quack,
With a baa-baa here,
And a baa-baa there,
Here a baa, there a baa, everywhere a baa-baa,
With a moo-moo here,
And a moo-moo there,
Here a moo, there a moo, everywhere a moo-moo,
Old Macdonald had a farm,
E-I-E-I-O!

HICKORY, DICKORY, DOCK

Hickory, dickory, dock,
The mouse ran up the clock.
The clock struck one,
The mouse ran down,
Hickory, dickory, dock.

Mary Had a Little Lamb

Mary had a little lamb
Its fleece was white as snow;
And everywhere that Mary went
The lamb was sure to go.

It followed her to school one day,
That was against the rule;
It made the children laugh and play
To see a lamb at school.

And so the teacher turned it out,
But still it lingered near,
And waited patiently about
Till Mary did appear.

Why does the lamb love Mary so?
The eager children cry;
Why, Mary loves the lamb, you know,
The teacher did reply.

HALFWAY DOWN

Halfway down the stairs
Is a stair
Where I sit.
There isn't any
Other stair
Quite like
It.

I'm not at the bottom,
I'm not at the top;
So this is the stair
Where
I always
Stop.

Halfway up the stairs
Isn't up,
And isn't down.
It isn't in the nursery,
It isn't in the town.
And all sorts of funny thoughts
Run round my head:
"It isn't really
Anywhere!
It's somewhere else
Instead!"

A. A. Milne

PAT-A-CAKE, PAT-A-CAKE

Pat-a-cake, pat-a-cake, baker's man,
Bake me a cake as fast as you can;
Pat it and prick it, and mark it with B,
Put it in the oven for Baby and me.

Spot's First Picnic

Eric Hill

"They'll be here any minute, Mom!" Spot was going on his first picnic with Tom, Helen, and Steve, and he was very excited.

He squeezed three jam sandwiches into his backpack.
"I hope I haven't forgotten anything," said Spot as he licked his sticky paws.
Then he had an idea.

"Just what we need for our picnic!"
shouted Spot. And before Sally could stop
him, Spot had pulled the tablecloth off the
table – and everything with it. *Crash!*

A knock at the door saved Spot from getting into more trouble.

"Your friends are here, Spot," Sally called. Spot rushed to the door.

"Oh, great! Let's go. 'Bye, Mom!"

Hi!

Sally looked up at the sky. It was cloudy. "Be careful," she told them. "And come back if it rains."

"Don't worry," said Helen. "I'll be in charge."

Have fun.

We will.

They climbed up a hill and Spot pointed to a small wood on the other side.

"Let's go there," he said. "I know where there's a stream and a big tree we can sit under for our picnic. Come on. I'll race you to the stream!"

Spot got there first. Steve was second and Helen came in third.

Tom panted up last, but when he saw the water, he was the first one in. *Splash!*

Aaahh!

15

"It was silly of you to jump in like that, Tom," Helen scolded. "You might have hurt yourself."

"Well, I didn't," said Tom. "I'm cool now. Let's go and eat."

Spot, Helen, and Steve crossed the stream on stepping stones.

I'm hungry.

Spot put down the tablecloth and unpacked the food.

Oh, no!

They had just started to eat when it began to rain.

"Quick, everyone," Helen shouted. "Put the tablecloth over the branch and make a tent."

It was cozy and dry under the tablecloth, but Steve stayed outside.

"It's only a shower," he said as he climbed up on a branch.

Suddenly Spot heard Steve shout, "Ooops!" and the tent began to shake.

Then everything went dark.

Good idea, Helen.

Steve had slipped off the branch and pulled the tent down on top of everyone.

"That's the end of our picnic," moaned Spot.

"It's all your fault, Steve," Helen complained. "You and your silly monkey tricks."

"We may as well go home," said Spot.

Sorry.

They packed up and started back across the stream.
But the stones were slippery from the rain and Helen lost
her balance.

   "Help!" she cried. They all tried to catch Helen, but
she fell and pulled everyone into the water with her.

What a mess! Spot looked around and laughed. "That was your fault, Helen. You and your silly balancing tricks!"
Everyone started giggling, and Helen laughed too.
"Wait until Mom sees us," Spot said.

Sally had a surprise ready for them when they got home.

"I knew you'd come back wet and hungry so I made you an indoor picnic."

"Thanks, Mom!" said Spot. "We are starving. We didn't mind getting wet at all, but we did mind eating soggy sandwiches!"

Ride a Cock Horse

Ride a cock horse
To Banbury Cross,
To see a fine lady
Upon a white horse.
With rings on her fingers
And bells on her toes,
She shall have music
Wherever she goes.

GEORGIE PORGIE

Georgie Porgie, pudding and pie,
Kissed the girls and made them cry;
When the boys came out to play,
Georgie Porgie ran away.

If You're Happy and You Know It, Clap Your Hands

If you're happy and you know it, clap your hands.
If you're happy and you know it, clap your hands.
If you're happy and you know it and you surely want to show it,
If you're happy and you know it, clap your hands.

If you're happy and you know it, nod your head.
If you're happy and you know it, nod your head.
If you're happy and you know it and you surely want to show it,
If you're happy and you know it, nod your head.

If you're happy and you know it, stamp your feet.
If you're happy and you know it, stamp your feet.
If you're happy and you know it and you surely want to show it,
If you're happy and you know it, stamp your feet.

If you're happy and you know it, say "we are."
If you're happy and you know it, say "we are."
If you're happy and you know it and you surely want to show it,
If you're happy and you know it, say "we are."

If you're happy and you know it, do all four.
If you're happy and you know it, do all four.
If you're happy and you know it and you surely want to show it,
If you're happy and you know it, do all four.

BRAHMS'S LULLABY

Lullaby and goodnight
With rosy bed light,
With down overspread
Is baby's sweet bed.

Lay you down now and rest,
May your slumbers be blest,
Lay you down now and rest,
May your slumbers be blest.

Johannes Brahms

GOLDEN SLUMBERS

Golden slumbers kiss your eyes,
Smiles awake you when you rise:
Sleep, pretty darling, do not cry,
And I will sing a lullaby:
Lullaby, lullaby, lullaby.

Thomas Dekker

INCY WINCY SPIDER

Incy Wincy spider climbed up the water spout
Down came the rain and washed the spider out.
Out came the sunshine and dried up all the rain,
So Incy Wincy spider climbed up the spout again.

It's Raining, It's Pouring

*I*t's raining, it's pouring,
The old man is snoring;
He went to bed and bumped his head
And couldn't get up in the morning!

LITTLE BO PEEP

Little Bo Peep has lost her sheep
And doesn't know where to find them.
Leave them alone and they'll come home
Bringing their tails behind them.

THE
THREE LITTLE
PIGS

Once upon a time there were three little pigs who lived in a very small house with their mother.

One day their mother gathered them all together and said, "It is time that you left our little house and built your own homes."

The three little pigs said good-bye to their mother and as they set off down the road she called after them, "Beware the wolf doesn't catch you and eat you!"

Soon they met a man who was carrying some straw.

"May I have some of your straw?" said the first

little pig. "I want to build a straw house for myself."

So the man gave the first little pig some straw to build a house.

"Now I am sure to be safe from the wolf," said the first little pig.

The other two little pigs went on their way, and soon they met a man who was carrying some sticks.

"May I have some of your sticks?" said the second little pig. "I want to build a wooden house for myself."

So the man gave the second little pig some sticks to build a house.

"Now I am sure to be safe from the wolf," said the second little pig.

The third little pig continued down the road by himself. Soon he met a man who was carrying some bricks.

"May I have some of your bricks?" said the third little pig. "I want to build a brick house for myself."

So the man gave the third little pig some bricks to build a house.

"Now I am sure to be safe from the wolf," said the third little pig.

The very next day the wolf came to the first little pig's house of straw.

"Little pig, little pig, let me come in," cried the wolf.

But the first little pig replied, "No, not by the hair of my chinny chin chin. You may not come in."

"Then I'll huff and I'll puff and I'll blow your house down!" said the wolf.

So he huffed and he puffed and he huffed and he puffed. The house of straw fell to pieces, and the wolf ate up the first little pig.

The next day the wolf came to the second little pig's house of sticks. "Little pig, little pig, let me come in," he cried.

But the second little pig replied, "No, not by the hair of my chinny chin chin. You may not come in."

"Then I'll huff and I'll puff and I'll blow your

house down!" said the wolf. So he huffed and he puffed and he huffed and he puffed. The house of sticks fell to pieces, and the wolf ate up the second little pig.

The next day the wolf came to the third little pig's house of bricks. "Little pig, little pig, let me come in," he cried.

But the third little pig replied, "No, not by the hair of my chinny chin chin. You may not come in."

"Then I'll huff and I'll puff and I'll blow your house down!" said the wolf.

So he huffed and he puffed and he huffed and he puffed. But the steadfast house of bricks did *not* fall down!

The wolf was very annoyed but then he had an idea. "Be ready at six o'clock tomorrow morning, little pig, and I shall take you to Farmer Jones's field to find some delicious truffles."

The little pig said that he would be ready at six o'clock. But the little pig was very clever and he knew that the wolf really wanted to eat him. So the next morning he set off an hour earlier at *five* o'clock. The little pig ran all the way to Farmer Jones's field, filled his basket with truffles and hurried home.

When the wolf arrived at the pig's house to find he'd been tricked, he was very cross.

But then the wolf had another idea. "Be ready at five o'clock tomorrow morning," he said to the little pig, "and I shall take you to Farmer Edwards's oak tree to gather some tasty acorns."

The little pig said that he would be ready at five o'clock. But instead, he set off at *four* o'clock the next morning. He ran all the way to Farmer Edwards's oak tree. He had already climbed to the top of the tree and begun to collect acorns when the wolf found him there.

The little pig saw the wolf coming and he threw an acorn as far as he could. The wolf ran after it. In a flash, the little pig jumped down from the tree and raced home as fast as he could.

When the wolf found out that he had been outwitted again, he was furious. He went to the little pig's house and banged on the door.

"Little pig, little pig," he cried, "I am going to climb down your chimney and eat you up! *You won't escape me this time!*"

The little pig was very, very frightened indeed. What could he do? He thought and thought and then he had an idea. He hurriedly put a huge pot of water on the fire to boil and waited.

The wolf clambered awkwardly down the chimney. "I'm coming to get you, little pig!" the wolf yelled in triumph. But as there was no lid on the little pig's pot, the wolf tumbled with a splash right into the boiling water.

And that was the end of the wolf!

Rub-a-Dub-Dub

Rub-a-dub-dub,
Three men in a tub,
And who do you think they are?
The butcher, the baker,
The candlestick maker;
Turn 'em out, knaves all three!

HUMPTY DUMPTY

Humpty Dumpty sat on the wall,
Humpty Dumpty had a great fall.
All the King's horses and all the King's men
Couldn't put Humpty together again.

GO TO BED LATE

Go to bed late
Stay very small,
Go to bed early
Grow very tall.

HERE WE GO ROUND
THE MULBERRY BUSH

Here we go round the mulberry bush,
The mulberry bush, the mulberry bush,
Here we go round the mulberry bush,
On a cold and frosty morning.

This is the way we wash our hands,
Wash our hands, wash our hands,
This is the way we wash our hands,
On a cold and frosty morning.

This is the way we brush our hair,
Brush our hair, brush our hair,
This is the way we brush our hair,
On a cold and frosty morning.

This is the way we go to school,
Go to school, go to school,
This is the way we go to school,
On a cold and frosty morning.

This is the way we wave bye-bye,
Wave bye-bye, wave bye-bye,
This is the way we wave bye-bye,
On a cold and frosty morning.

THREE LITTLE SPECKLED FROGS

Three little speckled frogs
Sat on a speckled log
Eating a most delicious lunch – yum yum!
One jumped into the pool
Where it was nice and cool,
Then there were two green speckled frogs – glub glub!

Two little speckled frogs
Sat on a speckled log
Eating a most delicious lunch – yum yum!
One jumped into the pool
Where it was nice and cool,
Then there was one green speckled frog – glub glub!

One little speckled frog
Sat on a speckled log
Eating a most delicious lunch – yum yum!
She jumped into the pool
Where it was nice and cool,
Then there were no green speckled frogs – glub glub!

THE SUN DESCENDING IN THE WEST

The sun descending in the west
The evening star does shine,
The birds are silent in their nest
And I must seek for mine,
The moon like a flower,
In heaven's high bower,
With silent delight
Sits and smiles on the night.

William Blake

The Tale of Tom Kitten

Beatrix Potter

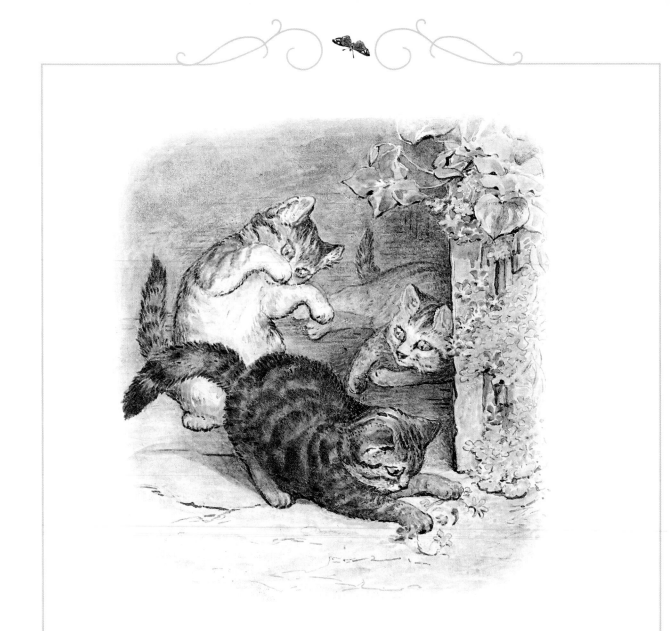

Once upon a time there were three little kittens, and their names were Mittens, Tom Kitten, and Moppet.

They had dear little fur coats of their own; and they tumbled about the doorstep and played in the dust.

But one day their mother—Mrs. Tabitha Twitchit—
expected friends to tea; so she fetched the kittens
indoors, to wash and dress them, before the fine
company arrived.

First she scrubbed
their faces (this one
is Moppet).

Then she brushed
their fur, (this one
is Mittens).

Then she combed
their tails and
whiskers (this is
Tom Kitten).
Tom was very
naughty, and he
scratched.

48

Mrs. Tabitha dressed Moppet and Mittens in clean pinafores and tuckers; and then she took all sorts of elegant uncomfortable clothes out of a chest of drawers, in order to dress up her son Thomas.

Tom Kitten was very fat, and he had grown; several buttons burst off. His mother sewed them on again.

When the three kittens were ready, Mrs. Tabitha unwisely turned them out into the garden, to be out of the way while she made hot buttered toast.

"Now keep your frocks clean, children! You must walk on your hind legs. Keep away from the dirty ash-pit, and from Sally Henny Penny, and from the pig-stye and the Puddle-Ducks."

Moppet and Mittens walked down the garden path unsteadily. Presently they trod upon their pinafores and fell on their noses.

When they stood up there were several green smears!

"Let us climb up the rockery, and sit on the garden wall," said Moppet.

They turned their pinafores back to front, and went up with a skip and a jump; Moppet's white tucker fell down into the road.

Tom Kitten was
quite unable to jump
when walking upon
his hind legs in
trousers. He came up
the rockery by
degrees, breaking the
ferns, and shedding
buttons right and left.

He was all in
pieces when he
reached the top
of the wall.

Moppet and
Mittens tried to
pull him together;
his hat fell off,
and the rest of
his buttons burst.

While they were in difficulties, there was a pit pat
paddle pat! and the three Puddle-Ducks came along
the hard high road, marching one behind the other
and doing the goose step—pit pat paddle pat!
pit pat waddle pat!

They stopped and stood in a row, and stared up at
the kittens. They had very small eyes and looked
surprised.

Then the two
duck-birds,
Rebeccah and
Jemima Puddle-
Duck, picked up
the hat and tucker
and put them on.

Mittens laughed
so that she fell off
the wall.

Moppet and Tom
descended after her;
the pinafores and all
the rest of Tom's
clothes came off on
the way down.

"Come! Mr. Drake
Puddle-Duck," said
Moppet—"Come
and help us to dress
him! Come and
button up Tom!"

Mr. Drake Puddle-Duck advanced in a slow sideways manner, and picked up the various articles.

But he put them on *himself*! They fitted him even worse than Tom Kitten.

"It's a very fine morning!" said Mr. Drake Puddle-Duck.

And he and Jemima and Rebeccah Puddle-Duck set off up the road, keeping step—pit pat, paddle pat! pit pat, waddle pat!

Then Tabitha Twitchit came down the garden and found her kittens on the wall with no clothes on.

She pulled them off the wall, smacked them, and took them back to the house.

"My friends will arrive in a minute, and you are not fit to be seen; I am affronted," said Mrs. Tabitha Twitchit.

She sent them upstairs; and I am sorry to say she told her friends that they were in bed with the measles; which was not true.

Quite the contrary; they were not in bed: *not* in the least.

Somehow there were very extraordinary noises over-head, which disturbed the dignity and repose of the tea party.

And I think that some day I shall have to make another, larger, book, to tell you more about Tom Kitten!

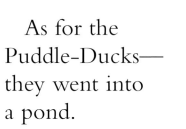

As for the
Puddle-Ducks—
they went into
a pond.

The clothes all
came off directly,
because there
were no buttons.

And Mr. Drake
Puddle-Duck,
and Jemima and
Rebeccah, have
been looking for
them ever since.

Ring-a-Ring o' Roses

Ring-a-ring o' roses,
A pocket full of posies.
A-tishoo! A-tishoo!
We all fall down.

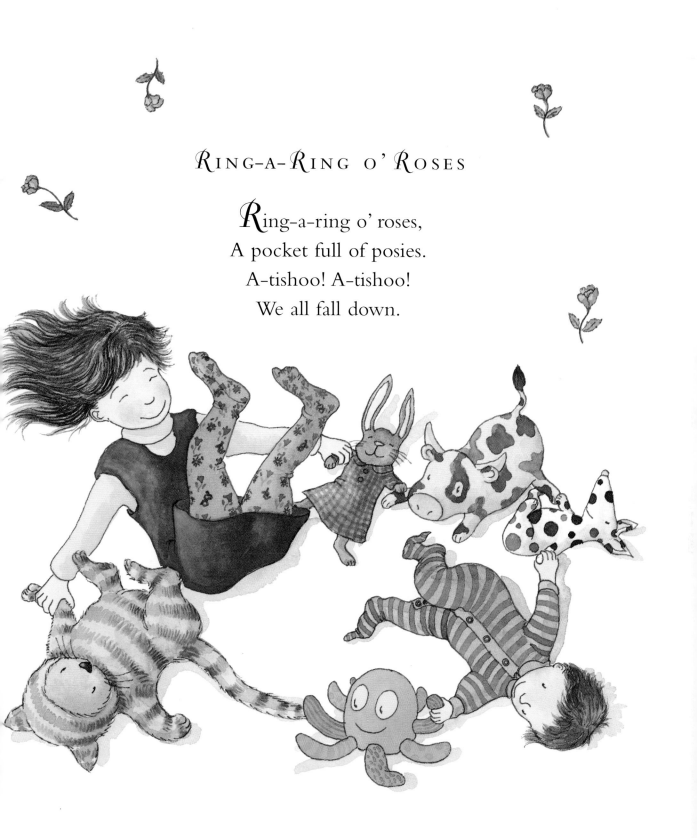

SING A SONG OF SIXPENCE

Sing a song of sixpence,
A pocket full of rye;
Four-and-twenty blackbirds
Baked in a pie.
When the pie was opened
The birds began to sing;
Wasn't that a dainty dish
To set before the King?

The King was in his counting house
Counting out his money;
The Queen was in the parlor
Eating bread and honey;
The maid was in the garden
Hanging out the clothes,
When down flew a blackbird
And pecked off her nose.

SONG

Where did you come from, baby dear?
Out of everywhere into here.

Where did you get your eyes so blue?
Out of the sky as I came through.

Where did you get that little tear?
I found it waiting when I got here.

What makes your forehead so smooth and high?
A soft hand stroked it as I went by.

What makes your cheek like a warm white rose?
I saw something better than anyone knows.

George MacDonald

HAPPY THOUGHT

The world is so full
of a number of things,
I'm sure we should all
be as happy as kings.

Robert Louis Stevenson

DOCTOR FOSTER

Doctor Foster went to Gloucester
In a shower of rain;
He stepped in a puddle,
Right up to his middle,
And never went there again.

One, Two, Buckle My Shoe

One, two,
Buckle my shoe;
Three, four,
Knock at the door;
Five, six,
Pick up sticks;
Seven, eight,
Lay them straight;
Nine, ten,
A big fat hen;
Eleven, twelve,
Dig and delve;
Thirteen, fourteen,
Maids a-courting;
Fifteen, sixteen,
Maids in the kitchen;
Seventeen, eighteen,
Maids in waiting;
Nineteen, twenty,
My plate's empty.

WEE WILLIE WINKIE

Wee Willie Winkie runs through the town,
Upstairs and downstairs in his nightgown,
Rapping at the window, crying through the lock,
Are the children in their beds?
For now it's eight o'clock.

GOLDILOCKS
AND THE
THREE BEARS

Once upon a time, there were three bears who lived in a cozy cottage with a little wooden door and shutters, right in the middle of the big, dark forest.

There was great big Father Bear, who was very fond of eating and sleeping. And there was medium-sized Mother Bear, who was very merry and wise. And there was little tiny Baby Bear, who sometimes cried, but then, after all, he was a very little bear.

One sunny morning, Mother Bear made a big pot of porridge for breakfast. She put it into three bowls and placed them on the kitchen table.

"That looks good," said Father Bear.

"It is good," said Mother Bear.

"Yum, yum," said Baby Bear.

But when they tasted it the three bears discovered that the porridge was much, much too hot to eat.

"We will leave it to cool down while we go out for our early morning walk," said Father Bear. "When we come back, it will be ready to eat." So off they went into the forest.

On the edge of the forest there lived a very naughty, mischievous little girl. She was called Goldilocks because she had long, golden hair down to her waist.

That morning Goldilocks's mother told her to go out into the forest and play.

"But don't go too far!" she said. "And don't get into mischief!"

But naughty Goldilocks went right into the heart of the forest, and there she came across the three bears' pretty little cottage.

"Oh, what a sweet little house! And the door is wide open. I'll just have a peep inside," she said to herself.

So she tiptoed up to the door and, seeing that no one was there, she stepped into the kitchen.

As soon as she saw the porridge on the table, Goldilocks rushed over to taste it. "I do feel hungry, and it smells so delicious," she said. So she picked up a big spoon and dipped it into Father Bear's bowl. "I'll just have a few spoonfuls," she said to herself.

But the porridge in Father Bear's big bowl was still too hot. And when she tried the porridge in Mother Bear's medium-sized bowl she found that was too lumpy.

At last she tried Baby Bear's porridge. It wasn't too hot. It wasn't too lumpy. It was just right! Goldilocks ate up every spoonful!

After that, Goldilocks felt very full. "I need to sit down!" she said. So she climbed up into Father Bear's chair. But it was much too high for her. Then she sat in Mother Bear's medium-sized chair. "This one is much too hard!" she grumbled. At last she found Baby Bear's tiny little chair with the letters BB carved into the back of it. It wasn't too high. It wasn't too hard. It was just right!

Goldilocks curled up happily in Baby Bear's chair. But she was far too heavy for such a little chair. With a terrible crash, the legs collapsed and the back fell off, and Goldilocks found herself sitting on the floor.

"Fiddlesticks!" said Goldilocks. "None of these chairs is any good. I shall have to find somewhere to lie down."

And she marched straight upstairs to the bedroom. She tried lying down in Father Bear's big bed, but that was far too hard.

Then she tried lying down in Mother Bear's medium-sized bed, but that was far too soft!

So she lay down on Baby Bear's bed. It wasn't too hard. It wasn't too soft. It was just right!

"Oh! This is very comfortable," sighed Goldilocks, snuggling into the little bed. And she fell asleep right away!

Just then the three bears arrived home hungry from their early morning walk.

"I'm ready for my breakfast *right this minute*," said Father Bear as they stepped through the front door. But when he sat down at the table he cried out in surprise, "Someone's been eating my porridge!"

"And someone's been eating *my* porridge," said Mother Bear. "I wonder why they didn't finish it?" she said, looking at her bowl.

"They must have liked mine!" cried Baby Bear, holding out his empty bowl. "Someone's been eating my porridge, and they've eaten all of it!" And tears sprang to his eyes.

"Look!" said Father Bear, pointing at his big chair. "Someone's been sitting in my chair!"

"And someone's been sitting in *my* chair," said Mother Bear.

"Someone's been sitting in my chair," wailed poor little Baby Bear, "and they've broken it all to pieces!"

"There, there, poor little Baby Bear," soothed

Mother Bear, "we'll get to the bottom of this."

The three bears began to search the house. They went upstairs to look around. "Someone's been sleeping in my bed!" said Father Bear.

"And someone's been sleeping in *my* bed," cried Mother Bear, "and they've left it in quite a mess!"

"Oh!" whimpered Baby Bear. "Someone's been sleeping in my bed and she's *still there*!" And he burst into tears.

At the sound of Baby Bear's voice, Goldilocks woke up with a start. The first thing she saw was Father Bear, looking very cross and baring his sharp teeth. And then she saw Mother Bear with her arms folded and tapping her foot. And then she saw Baby Bear weeping into his handkerchief. Goldilocks jumped up in fright. She ran down the stairs and out of the house and into the forest as fast as her legs could carry her.

"I don't think that naughty little girl will trouble us again," said Father Bear, smiling.

And she never, ever did.

THE WHEELS ON THE BUS

The wheels on the bus go round and round
Round and round
Round and round
The wheels on the bus go round and round
All day long.

The horn on the bus goes beep beep beep
Beep beep beep
Beep beep beep
The horn on the bus goes beep beep beep
All day long.

The lights on the bus go blink blink blink
Blink blink blink
Blink blink blink
The lights on the bus go blink blink blink
All day long.

The doors on the bus, they open and shut
Open and shut
Open and shut
The doors on the bus, they open and shut
All day long.

The babies on the bus go wah-wah-wah
Wah-wah-wah
Wah-wah-wah
The babies on the bus go wah-wah-wah
All day long.

The mommies on the bus go shh-shh-shh
Shh-shh-shh
Shh-shh-shh
The mommies on the bus go shh-shh-shh
All day long.

But the children on the bus go up and down
Up and down
Up and down
The children on the bus go up and down
All day long!

One, Two, Three, Four, Five

One, two, three, four, five,
Once I caught a fish alive,
Six, seven, eight, nine, ten,
Then I let it go again.
Why did you let it go?
Because it bit my finger so.
Which finger did it bite?
The little finger on the right.

My Baby

My baby has a mottled fist,
My baby has a neck in creases;
My baby kisses and is kissed,
For he's the very thing for kisses.

Christina Rossetti

A BABY-SERMON

The lightning and thunder
They go and they come;
But the stars and the stillness
Are always at home.

George MacDonald

The North Wind Doth Blow

The north wind doth blow,
And we shall have snow,
And what will poor Robin do then,
Poor thing?
He'll sit in a barn,
And keep himself warm,
And hide his head under his wing,
Poor thing.

STAR LIGHT, STAR BRIGHT

Star light, star bright,
First star I see tonight,
Wish I may,
Wish I might,
Have the wish I wish tonight.

PUSSY-CAT, PUSSY-CAT

Pussy-cat, pussy-cat, where have you been?
I've been up to London to visit the Queen.
Pussy-cat, pussy-cat, what did you there?
I frightened a little mouse under her chair.

Baa, Baa, Black Sheep

Baa, Baa, black sheep,
Have you any wool?
Yes, sir, yes, sir,
Three bags full;
One for the master,
And one for the dame,
And one for the little boy
Who lives down the lane.

THE OWL AND THE PUSSY-CAT

The Owl and the Pussy-cat went to sea
    In a beautiful pea-green boat,
They took some honey, and plenty of money,
    Wrapped up in a five-pound note.

The Owl looked up to the stars above,
And sang to a small guitar,
"O lovely Pussy! O Pussy, my love,
What a beautiful Pussy you are,
You are,
You are!
What a beautiful Pussy you are!"

Pussy said to the Owl, "You elegant fowl!
How charmingly sweet you sing!
O let us be married! too long we have tarried:
But what shall we do for a ring?"

They sailed away, for a year and a day,
To the land where the Bong-tree grows
And there in a wood a Piggy-wig stood
With a ring at the end of his nose,
His nose,
His nose,
With a ring at the end of his nose.

"Dear Pig, are you willing to sell for one shilling
Your ring?" Said the Piggy, "I will."
So they took it away, and were married next day
By the Turkey who lives on the hill.

They dined on mince, and slices of quince,
Which they ate with a runcible spoon;
And hand in hand, on the edge of the sand,
They danced by the light of the moon,
The moon,
The moon,
They danced by the light of the moon.

Edward Lear

The Farmer's in the Dell

The farmer's in the dell,
The farmer's in the dell,
E-I-E-I,
The farmer's in the dell.

The farmer wants a wife,
The farmer wants a wife,
E-I-E-I,
The farmer wants a wife.

The wife wants a child,
The wife wants a child,
E-I-E-I,
The wife wants a child.

The child wants a nurse,
The child wants a nurse,
E-I-E-I,
The child wants a nurse.

The nurse wants a dog,
The nurse wants a dog,
E-I-E-I,
The nurse wants a dog.

We all pat the dog,
We all pat the dog,
E-I-E-I,
We all pat the dog.

I LOVE LITTLE PUSSY

I love little pussy,
Her coat is so warm,
And if I don't hurt her
She'll do me no harm.
So I'll not pull her tail,
Nor drive her away,
But pussy and I
Very gently will play.
She shall sit by my side,
And I'll give her some food;
And pussy will love me
Because I am good.

OLD KING COLE

Old King Cole
Was a merry old soul,
And a merry old soul was he;
He called for his pipe,
And he called for his bowl,
And he called for his fiddlers three.

Every fiddler he had a fiddle,
And a very fine fiddle had he;
Oh, there's none so rare
As can compare
With King Cole and his fiddlers three.

BED IN SUMMER

*I*n winter I get up at night
And dress by yellow candlelight.
In summer, quite the other way,
I have to go to bed by day.

I have to go to bed and see
The birds still hopping on the tree,
Or hear the grown-up people's feet
Still going past me in the street.

And does it not seem hard to you,
When all the sky is clear and blue,
And I should like so much to play,
To have to go to bed by day?

Robert Louis Stevenson

SPRING GOES, SUMMER COMES

*T*he little darling, Spring,
Has run away;
The sunshine grew too hot for her to stay.

She kissed her sister, Summer,
And she said:
"When I am gone, you must be queen instead."

Now reigns the Lady Summer,
Round whose feet
A thousand fairies flock with blossoms sweet.

Cicely Mary Barker

THREE LITTLE MONKEYS

Three little monkeys jumping on the bed
One fell off and bumped his head.
Mommy called the doctor and the doctor said,
"No more monkeys jumping on the bed!"

Two little monkeys jumping on the bed
One fell off and bumped his head.
Mommy called the doctor and the doctor said,
"No more monkeys jumping on the bed!"

One little monkey jumping on the bed
He fell off and bumped his head.
Mommy called the doctor and the doctor said,
"No more monkeys jumping on the bed!"

I'm a Little Teapot

I'm a little teapot,
Short and stout,
Here's my handle,
Here's my spout.
When the kettle's boiling
Hear me shout:
Tip me up
And pour me out!

THE
THREE BILLY
GOATS GRUFF

Three goats once lived together in a field. The littlest one was called Little Billy Goat Gruff. The next one was bigger than Little Billy Goat Gruff, so he was called Big Billy Goat Gruff. But the third was the biggest of them all, and he was called Great Big Billy Goat Gruff.

At the end of their field was a river, and across the river was another field. Now this field was empty and the grass there grew rich and long and very green. Little Billy Goat Gruff said he could see some beautiful rosy apples on a tree over in the field. Big Billy Goat Gruff said there was plenty of lovely

clover there. And Great Big Billy Goat Gruff said he
had seen ripe red berries growing there as well. They
all longed to cross the river.

There was a low bridge that crossed the river
between the two fields, but under it there lived a
horrible troll who liked to eat goats better than
anything else. So the three Billy Goats Gruff never
dared to cross the bridge into the lovely empty field
in case the troll caught them.

One day Little Billy Goat Gruff felt very, very
hungry and he told his brothers, "I'm going to cross
over the bridge and eat some of those rosy apples."

His brothers said, "Be careful; remember the troll.
He's certain to catch you."

But Little Billy Goat Gruff was determined. Off he
went, trit-trot, trit-trot, over the bridge. "I'm too
small for him," he said.

When he was halfway across the bridge, the troll
suddenly put his head out and said, "Who's that
running, trit-trot, trit-trot, over my bridge?"

"It's only me, Little Billy Goat Gruff."

"I'm going to eat you up," said the troll.

But Little Billy Goat Gruff said, "Don't eat me,

because I'm only *Little* Billy Goat Gruff. I've got a brother called *Big* Billy Goat Gruff, who is much bigger and fatter than I am. Why don't you wait for him?"

"All right," growled the troll, "I will."

So Little Billy Goat Gruff trotted across the bridge to the other field and began to eat all the long green grass and the beautiful rosy apples.

Big Billy Goat Gruff saw that Little Billy Goat Gruff had got safely across; so off he went too, trit-trot, trit-trot, over the bridge.

When he was halfway across, the troll put his head out and said, "Who's that running, trit-trot, trit-trot, over my bridge?"

"It's only Big Billy Goat Gruff."

"Then I'm going to eat you up," growled the troll.

But Big Billy Goat Gruff said, "Don't eat me, because I'm only *Big* Billy Goat Gruff. I've got a brother called *Great* Big Billy Goat Gruff, who is still bigger and fatter than I am. Why don't you wait for him?"

"All right," grunted the troll, "I will."

So Big Billy Goat Gruff trotted across the bridge to the other side and began to feast on the long green grass and the lovely clover.

Great Big Billy Goat Gruff thought it was time he went over to join his brothers and have some of the long green grass and the ripe red berries. So off he went, trit-trot, trit-trot, over the bridge. When he was halfway across, the troll put out his head and said, "Who's that running, trit-trot, trit-trot, over my bridge?"

"It's Great Big Billy Goat Gruff."

"You're the one I'm going to gobble up," growled the troll. "I've been waiting for you."

Trying not to look frightened, Great Big Billy Goat Gruff said, "Oh, have you? You just try to gobble me up and see what happens."

Then the troll jumped up on

to the bridge, but Great Big Billy Goat Gruff put down his head, ran at the troll and knocked him off the bridge and into the river. Howling, the troll disappeared under the water and was drowned.

Great Big Billy Goat Gruff trotted across the bridge to the other side and joined Big Billy Goat Gruff and Little Billy Goat Gruff in their new field. They all ate the long green grass, and Great Big Billy Goat Gruff ate the ripe red berries, Big Billy Goat Gruff ate the lovely clover, and Little Billy Goat Gruff ate all the beautiful rosy apples. And they all grew very fat.

I Had a Little Nut Tree

I had a little nut tree,
Nothing would it bear
But a silver nutmeg
And a golden pear;
The King of Spain's daughter
Came to visit me,
And all for the sake
Of my little nut tree.

THIS LITTLE PIGGY

This little piggy went to market;
This little piggy stayed at home;
This little piggy had roast beef;
This little piggy had none;
And this little piggy cried, "Wee! Wee! Wee!"
All the way home.

LITTLE BOY BLUE

Little Boy Blue,
Come blow your horn,
The sheep's in the meadow,
The cow's in the corn.
Where is the boy
Who looks after the sheep?
He's under a haystack
Fast asleep.
Will you wake him?
No, not I,
For if I do,
He's sure to cry.

LONDON BRIDGE IS FALLING DOWN

London Bridge is falling down,
Falling down, falling down,
London Bridge is falling down,
My fair lady.

Build it up with wood and clay,
Wood and clay, wood and clay,
Build it up with wood and clay,
My fair lady.

Wood and clay will wash away,
Wash away, wash away,
Wood and clay will wash away,
My fair lady.

Build it up with bricks and mortar,
Bricks and mortar, bricks and mortar,
Build it up with bricks and mortar,
My fair lady.

Bricks and mortar will not stay,
Will not stay, will not stay,
Bricks and mortar will not stay,
My fair lady.

Build it up with iron and steel,
Iron and steel, iron and steel,
Build it up with iron and steel,
My fair lady.

Iron and steel will bend and bow,
Bend and bow, bend and bow,
Iron and steel will bend and bow,
My fair lady.

Build it up with silver and gold,
Silver and gold, silver and gold,
Build it up with silver and gold,
My fair lady.

Silver and gold will be stolen away,
Stolen away, stolen away,
Silver and gold will be stolen away,
My fair lady.

Good Night

Now good night.
Fold up your clothes
As you were taught,
Fold your two hands,
Fold up your thought;
Day is the plowland,
Night is the stream,
Day is for doing
And night is for dream.
Now good night.

Eleanor Farjeon

GOOD NIGHT, GOOD NIGHT

The dark is dreaming.
Day is done.
Good night, good night
To everyone.

Good night to the birds,
And the fish in the sea,
Good night to the bears
And good night to me.

Dennis Lee

SILVERLY

Silverly,
Silverly,
Over the
Trees
The moon drifts
By on a
Runaway
Breeze.

Dozily,
Dozily,
Deep in her
Bed,
A little girl
Dreams with the
Moon in her
Head.

Dennis Lee

The Snowman

The original pictures, with words, by

Raymond Briggs

In the morning James woke to see snow falling. He ran into the garden as fast as he could and started to make a snowman. He gave him a scarf and a hat, a tangerine for a nose, and lumps of coal for his buttons and his eyes.

What a wonderful snowman he was! James could not
go to sleep because he was thinking about him.

In the middle of the night he crept down to see the
snowman again.

Then suddenly . . . the snowman *moved*!
"Come in," said James. "But you must be very quiet."

The snowman was amazed by everything he saw.

They even went into James's mother and father's bedroom and the snowman dressed up in their clothes.

Suddenly, the snowman took James by the hand and ran out of the house, across the snow and up, up into the air.

They were flying!

James and the snowman flew for miles through the cold, moonlight air.

Then they landed gently on the snow, home safe in
the garden.

James gave the snowman a hug.

Then he said good night and went indoors.

In the morning he was woken up by bright sunlight shining on his face. He must see the snowman again! James ran out of his room, down the stairs, across the living room, past his mother and father, and into the garden.

Rock-a-Bye, Baby

Rock-a-bye, baby, on the tree top;
When the wind blows, the cradle will rock;
When the bough bends, the cradle will fall;
Down will come baby, cradle and all.

JACK AND JILL

Jack and Jill
Went up the hill,
To fetch a pail of water;

Jack fell down
And broke his crown,
And Jill came tumbling after.

DIDDLE, DIDDLE DUMPLING

Diddle, diddle dumpling,
my son John,
Went to bed with
his trousers on;
One shoe off
and one shoe on,
Diddle, diddle dumpling,
my son John.

Pop Goes the Weasel

Half a pound of tuppenny rice,
Half a pound of treacle,
That's the way the money goes,
Pop goes the weasel!

Up and down the city road,
In and out the eagle,
That's the way the money goes,
Pop goes the weasel!

Every night when I go out,
The monkey's on the table,
Take a stick and knock it off,
Pop goes the weasel!

A penny for a ball of thread,
Another for a needle,
That's the way the money goes,
Pop goes the weasel!

All around the cobbler's bench,
The monkey chased the people;
The donkey thought 'twas all in fun,
Pop goes the weasel!

POLLY PUT THE KETTLE ON

Polly put the kettle on,
Polly put the kettle on,
Polly put the kettle on,
We'll all have tea.

Sukey take it off again,
Sukey take it off again,
Sukey take it off again,
They've all gone away.

GROWING UP

I've got shoes with grown-up laces,
I've got knickers and a pair of braces,
I'm all ready to run some races.
Who's coming out with me?

I've got a nice new pair of braces,
I've got shoes with new brown laces,
I know wonderful paddly places.
Who's coming out with me?

Every morning my new grace is,
"Thank you, God, for my nice braces;
I can tie my new brown laces."
Who's coming out with me?

A. A. Milne

Lavender's Blue, Dilly, Dilly

Lavender's blue, dilly, dilly.
Lavender's green.
When I am king, dilly, dilly,
You shall be queen.

Call up your men, dilly, dilly.
Set them to work.
Some to the plough, dilly, dilly.
Some to the cart.

Some to make hay, dilly, dilly.
Some to thresh corn.
While you and I, dilly, dilly.
Keep ourselves warm.

HEADS AND SHOULDERS

Heads and shoulders, knees and toes, knees and toes,
Heads and shoulders, knees and toes, knees and toes,
And eyes and ears and mouth and nose,
Heads and shoulders, knees and toes, knees and toes.

The Grand Old Duke of York

Oh, the grand old Duke of York,
He had ten thousand men;
He marched them up to the top of the hill,
And he marched them down again.
And when they were up, they were up,
And when they were down, they were down,
And when they were only halfway up,
They were neither up nor down.

The Ugly Duckling

Based on the story by Hans Christian Andersen

Once upon a time, there was a duck. She lived on a farm and spent her days happily scratching for food in the farmyard with the other ducks and the chickens and swimming in the duckpond.

But one day, the duck felt restless. She couldn't settle to swimming in the pond or scratching for food as usual. "I know what I want!" she cried. "I want to lay some eggs!"

She didn't want all the other ducks to know, so she scrambled out under the farmyard gate and into the field beyond. She waddled off down to the river bank, and found a nice, quiet place where the grass was thick and lush and the rushes grew tall. "This is just the spot to build a nest. My eggs will be nice and safe here," she said.

Once the duck had laid her eggs, she had to sit on them to keep them warm for many days. Every so often, she left the nest to go down to the river for some food and a drink of water, but she always hurried back to her eggs as fast as she could.

Finally, the big day arrived – the eggs were ready to hatch! First one, then two, three, four chicks pecked their way out through the eggshell. The duck was so thrilled, she couldn't help quacking with excitement, "Oh, how little and yellow and beautiful you are! I shall be the envy of all the other ducks in the farmyard!"

But the fifth chick was different. He wasn't little or yellow. He was big and gray, and when he finally chipped his way out of the egg his mother was horrified. "Oh my goodness!" she sobbed. "What a very *ugly* duckling you are!"

The next day the mother duck took the five little chicks down to the river to teach them how to swim, then it was time to go back to the farmyard. Proudly, the mother duck introduced her new brood, and the other ducks agreed that the four little yellow chicks were very beautiful indeed.

But none of them liked the fifth chick at all. "He's so big!" "And gray!" "And *ugly*!" they said.

The ugly duckling tried to make friends, but no one would play with him or talk to him, not even his brothers and sisters. They all just laughed at him and said unkind things.

So he decided to run away. Early one morning, he squeezed under the gate and ran down to the river. Then he swam and swam and swam until he could swim

ha ha

ho ho

no more. Night was falling and he was miles away from home in the middle of a dark wood. He climbed out on to the river bank. It was cold and the poor little ugly duckling was frightened and lonely.

Then, as he huddled himself up under some leaves, he heard voices calling from the sky. Looking up, he saw some beautiful white swans flying overhead. "How lovely they are!" he thought to himself. "If only I could be like them!" And he fell fast asleep.

The next day, the ugly duckling was looking for food on the river, when some wild ducks came swimming up. "What an ugly duckling you are!" they said. "You can't stay here!" They pecked him with their sharp beaks until he ran away.

Soon, he was hopelessly lost in the wood. Rain was falling and the little ugly duckling was weak with hunger and tiredness, when he came across a cottage. There was a gap under the door just big enough for him to squeeze through.

Inside, he found a lovely warm fire with a cat and a hen and a little old lady in

hello there!

go away!

front of it. The little old lady gave the duckling some water to drink and some corn to eat and a cozy warm seat in front of the fire. "You can stay here as long as you like," she said.

But the cat and the hen were jealous of the little duckling. They didn't want to share their home with him, so one night they cornered him. "You can't purr and you can't lay eggs," they said. "What use are you to anyone? And you're ugly too. You can't stay here." Then they pushed him out of the door.

So the poor little duckling set off on his travels once more, out on to the great lonely marshland. But winter was falling, and as the weather got colder and colder, it grew harder and harder for the duckling to find food. One morning, a farmer came across the duckling half frozen on the ice. He took the duckling home to his wife, who fed him and looked after him until he was strong again.

But the farmer's children wanted to play with him.

They chased him and pulled his tail, until the duckling had to run away again.

The ugly duckling stayed hidden among the reeds through the rest of the long cold winter, until the spring sunshine fell brightly on the water. Then he stretched his wings and flew up into the sky and over the river.

Down below, he saw three lovely white swans swimming. "Come and join us!" they called. The duckling could hardly believe they were talking to him, but as he flew down, he caught sight of his own reflection in the river. He saw strong white wings and a long white neck and he realized that he wasn't an ugly duckling any more. He was a beautiful swan, just like the ones calling to him, and he would never be lonely again.

HUSH, LITTLE BABY

Hush, little baby, don't say a word,
Papa's going to buy you a mocking bird.

If the mocking bird won't sing,
Papa's going to buy you a diamond ring.

If the diamond ring turns to brass,
Papa's going to buy you a looking glass.

If the looking glass gets broke,
Papa's going to buy you a billy goat.

If that billy goat runs away,
Papa's going to buy you another today.

LITTLE JACK HORNER

Little Jack Horner, sat in the corner,
Eating a Christmas pie;
He put in his thumb, and pulled out a plum,
And said, oh! what a good boy am I.

Row, Row, Row Your Boat

Row, row, row your boat,
Gently down the stream.
Merrily, merrily, merrily, merrily;
Life is but a dream.

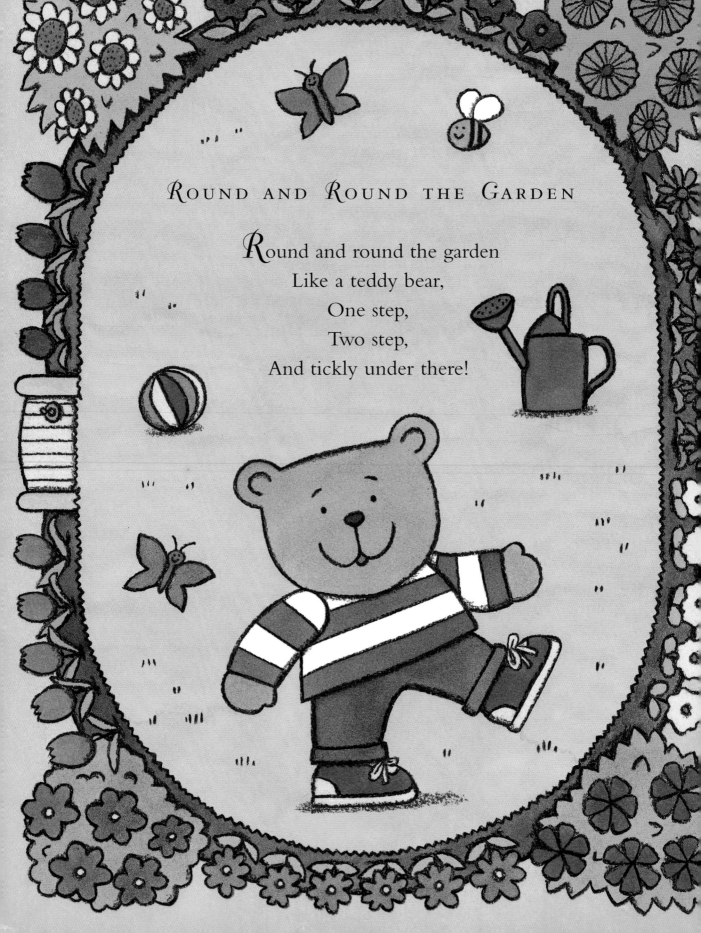

ROUND AND ROUND THE GARDEN

Round and round the garden
Like a teddy bear,
One step,
Two step,
And tickly under there!

Rain, Rain, Go Away

Rain, rain, go away,
Come again another day.

Dance to Your Daddy

Dance to your daddy,
My little babby,
Dance to your daddy,
My little lamb.

You shall have a fishy
In a little dishy,
You shall have a fishy
When the boat comes in.

Roses are Red

Roses are red,
Violets are blue,
Honey is sweet
And so are you.

This is the Way the Lady Rides

This is the way the lady rides,
Nim, nim, nim, nim,
This is the way the gentleman rides,
Trim, trim, trim, trim,
This is the way the farmer rides,
Trot, trot, trot, trot,
This is the way the huntsman rides,
A-gallop, a-gallop, a-gallop, a-gallop,
This is the way the old man rides,
Hobbledehoy, hobbledehoy, hobbledehoy,
And down into the ditch!

LUCY & TOM
AT THE
SEASIDE

Shirley Hughes

One hot day Lucy and Tom and their mom and dad thought they would go to the seaside.

Lucy is helping to pack up the picnic. There are sandwiches and hard-boiled eggs, apples, biscuits, and a bottle of orange squash. There is also a lovely chocolate cake.

Tom goes off to find the buckets and spades in the sandpit.

They go to the seaside in the train.

Tom keeps asking when they are going to get to the sea.

Lucy wears her armbands in the train so as to be all ready to swim when they get there.

At last they've arrived! They walk down a rather long road carrying all the picnic things and bathing bags and buckets and spades.

There's a very special seasidey smell.

And there's the sea!

It's much bigger than either Lucy or Tom had
ever remembered.

They run straight down to where the waves are coming up on to the wet sand and walk along the edge.

There are a lot of other children on the beach, as well as mothers and fathers and babies and grannies and people paddling, and dogs who dash in and out of the water, barking excitedly at seagulls.

Lucy and Tom want to swim right away, so
they all put on their bathing suits and go into
the sea, hand in hand. Lucy and Dad do some
swimming. The sea is much rougher and
splashier than the swimming pool near home.
It's harder to swim in, but much more fun.

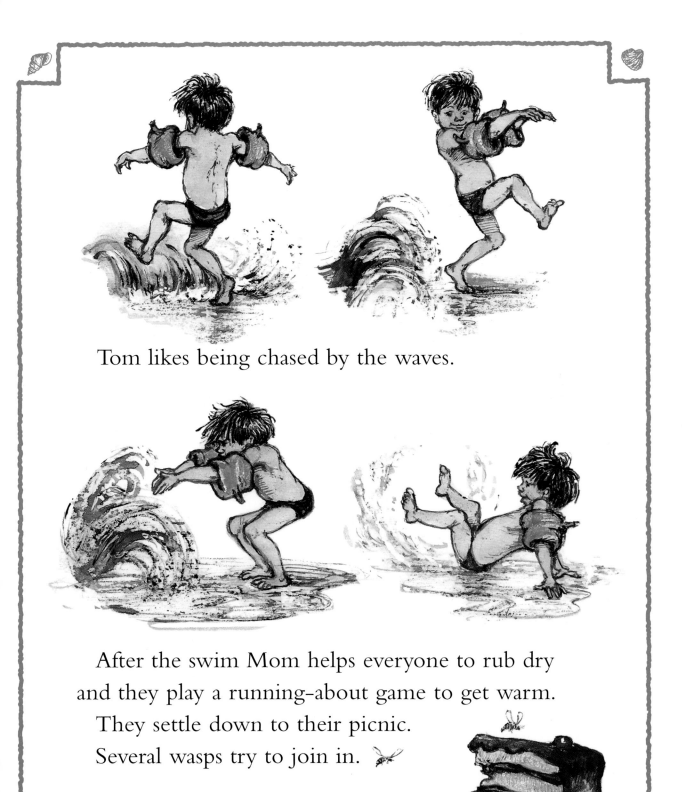

Tom likes being chased by the waves.

After the swim Mom helps everyone to rub dry
and they play a running-about game to get warm.
They settle down to their picnic.
Several wasps try to join in.

The tide is coming in.

Dad helps Lucy and Tom to make a beautiful sand castle. It has turrets covered in shells and stones, a moat, and a tunnel going right through the middle and coming out the other side.

Slowly the moat fills up with water, then the tunnel.
Soon only the top turret is left.
Then nothing at all.

A lot of interesting things are happening on the beach.

There are people flying kites and playing cricket and ball games.

Two little girls are burying their father's legs in the sand so that only his toes are sticking out.

Some people are trying to get in or out of their bathing suits under towels, which is very difficult.

Lucy and Tom play in a rock-pool.

Lucy finds lots of different kinds of seaweed and some shells which she puts into her bucket.

Tom finds some stones and a crab's claw.

Lucy makes a face in the sand. It has stones for eyes, a row of little shells for teeth, and a lot of seaweedy hair.

Mom helps Tom make a speedboat pointing right out to sea.

Further up the beach there are some donkeys.
Lucy and Tom ask if they can have a ride.

Lucy's donkey is gray with white legs. His name –
"Pepsi" – is written on his harness.

Tom's donkey is brown and is called "Cola."

It's nearly time to go home. Mom is packing up the
picnic things. There's just time for a last ice-cream.

Lucy writes her name in very big letters in the
wet sand.

Then she writes Tom's name too.

It's been a *lovely* day.

Two Little Dicky Birds

Two little dicky birds
Sitting on a wall;
One named Peter,
The other named Paul.
Fly away, Peter!
Fly away, Paul!
Come back, Peter!
Come back, Paul!

THERE WAS A LITTLE GIRL

There was a little girl, and she had a little curl,
Right in the middle of her forehead;
When she was good, she was very, very good,
But when she was bad, she was horrid!

I SEE THE MOON

I see the moon,
And the moon sees me;
God bless the moon,
And God bless me.

Five Little Ducks

Five little ducks went swimming one day,
Over the pond and far away.
Mother Duck said, "Quack, quack, quack, quack."
But only four little ducks came back.

Four little ducks went swimming one day,
Over the pond and far away.
Mother Duck said, "Quack, quack, quack, quack."
But only three little ducks came back.

Three little ducks went swimming one day,
Over the pond and far away.
Mother Duck said, "Quack, quack, quack, quack."
But only two little ducks came back.

Two little ducks went swimming one day,
Over the pond and far away.
Mother Duck said, "Quack, quack, quack, quack."
But only one little duck came back.

One little duck went swimming one day,
Over the pond and far away.
Mother Duck said, "Quack, quack, quack, quack."
And five little ducks came swimming back.

Wyn Daniel

Horsie, Horsie

Horsie, horsie, don't you stop,
Just let your feet go clippetty clop;
Your tail goes swish, and the wheels go round –
Giddy up, you're homeward bound!

THE GINGERBREAD MAN

Once upon a time there was a little old woman and a little old man, and they lived all alone. They were very happy together, but they wanted a child and since they had none, they decided to make one out of gingerbread. So one day the little old woman and the little old man made themselves a little gingerbread man, and they put him in the oven to bake.

When the gingerbread man was done, the little old woman opened the oven door and pulled out the pan. Out jumped the little gingerbread man – and away he ran. The little old woman and the little old man ran after him as fast as they could, but he just laughed and said, "Run, run, as fast as you can. You can't catch me! I'm the Gingerbread Man!"

And they couldn't catch him.

The gingerbread man ran on and on until he came to a cow.

"Stop, little gingerbread man," said the cow. "I want to eat you."

But the gingerbread man said, "I have run away from a little old woman and a little old man, and I can run away from you, too. I can, I can!"

And the cow began to chase the gingerbread man, but the gingerbread man ran faster, and said, "Run, run, as fast as you can. You can't catch me! I'm the Gingerbread Man!"

And the cow couldn't catch him.

The gingerbread man ran on until he came to a horse.

"Please, stop, little gingerbread man," said the horse. "I want to eat you."

And the gingerbread man said, "I have run away from a little old woman, a little old man, and a cow, and I can run away from you, too. I can, I can!"

And the horse began to chase the gingerbread man, but the gingerbread man ran faster and called to the horse, "Run, run, as fast as you can. You can't catch me! I'm the Gingerbread Man!"

And the horse couldn't catch him.

By and by the gingerbread man came to a field full of farmers.

"Stop," said the farmers. "Don't run so fast. We want to eat you."

But the gingerbread man said, "I have run away from a little old woman, a little old man, a cow, and a horse, and I can run away from you, too. I can, I can!"

And the farmers began to chase him, but the gingerbread man ran faster than ever and said, "Run, run, as fast as you can. You can't catch me! I'm the Gingerbread Man!"

And the farmers couldn't catch him.

The gingerbread man ran faster and faster. He ran past a school full of children.

"Stop, little gingerbread man," said the children. "We want to eat you."

But the gingerbread man said, "I have run away from a little old woman, a little old man, a cow, a horse, and a field full of farmers, and I can run away from you, too. I can, I can!"

And the children began to chase him, but the gingerbread man ran faster as he said, "Run, run, as fast as you can. You can't catch me! I'm the Gingerbread Man!"

And the children couldn't catch him.

By this time the gingerbread man was so proud of himself he didn't think anyone could catch him. Pretty soon he saw a fox. The fox looked at him and began to run after him. But the gingerbread man said, "You can't catch me! I have run away from a little old woman, a little old man, a cow, a horse, a field full of farmers, a school full of children, and I can run away from you, too. I can, I can! Run, run, as fast as you can. You can't catch me! I'm the Gingerbread Man!"

"Oh," said the fox, "I do not want to catch you. I only want to help you run away."

Just then the gingerbread man came to a river. He could not swim across, and he had to keep running.

"Jump on my tail," said the fox. "I will take you across."

So the gingerbread man jumped on the fox's tail, and the fox began to swim across the river. When he had gone a little way, he said to the gingerbread man, "You are too heavy on my tail. Jump on my back."

And the gingerbread man did.

The fox swam a little further, and then he said, "I am afraid you will get wet on my back. Jump on my shoulder."

And the gingerbread man did.

In the middle of the river, the fox said, "Oh dear, my shoulder is sinking. Jump on my nose, and I can hold you out of the water."

So the little gingerbread man jumped on the fox's nose, and the fox threw back his head and snapped his sharp teeth.

"Oh dear," said the gingerbread man, "I am a quarter gone!"

Next minute he said, "Now I am half gone!"

And next minute he said, "Oh, my goodness gracious! I am three quarters gone!"

And then the gingerbread man never said anything more at all.

OATS AND BEANS AND BARLEY GROW

Oats and beans and barley grow,
Oats and beans and barley grow,
Do you or I or anyone know
How oats and beans and barley grow?

First the farmer sows his seed,
Then he stands and takes his ease,
He stamps his foot and claps his hand
And turns around to view the land.

I Saw a Ship a-Sailing

I saw a ship a-sailing,
A-sailing on the sea,
And oh, but it was laden
With pretty things for thee!

There were comfits in the cabin,
And apples in the hold;
The sails were made of silk,
And the masts were all of gold.

The four-and-twenty sailors
That stood between the decks
Were four-and-twenty white mice
With chains about their necks.

The captain was a duck
With a packet on his back,
And when the ship began to move
The captain said, "Quack! Quack!"

TWINKLE, TWINKLE, LITTLE STAR

Twinkle, twinkle, little star,
How I wonder what you are!
Up above the world so high,
Like a diamond in the sky.